ALIEN IN MY POCKET

Ohm vs. Amp

by
Nate Ball

illustrated by
Macky Pamintuan

HARPER
An Imprint of HarperCollins Publishers

Alien in My Pocket: Ohm vs. Amp

Text by Nate Ball, copyright © 2014 by HarperCollins Publishers

Illustrations by Macky Pamintuan, copyright © 2014 by HarperCollins Publishers

All rights reserved. Printed in the United States of America.

No part of this book may be used or reproduced in any manner whatsoever without written permission except in the case of brief quotations embodied in critical articles and reviews. For information address HarperCollins Children's Books, a division of HarperCollins Publishers, 195 Broadway, New York, NY 10007.

www.harpercollinschildrens.com

Library of Congress catalog card number: 2014034089

ISBN 978-0-06-231489-5 (trade bdg.)—ISBN 978-0-06-221631-1 (pbk.)

Typography by Jeff Shake

15 16 17 18 19   OPM   10 9 8 7 6 5 4 3 2 1

❖

First Edition

Contents

01

My Secret Roommate

When a pint-size alien from outer space crash-lands his spaceship on your bed during the middle of the night, your life can get pretty messed up.

You can never go back to the way it was.

My little blue alien and I argued constantly for two straight months as we tried to repair his junky ship. We fought like two crabs in a bucket.

Then we ran out of steam.

And we learned to get along.

I guess you can get used to most things that at first seem to be the absolute ruin of your life, like summer school, tuna fish, and spelling quizzes.

I had grown comfortable with Amp, and he had gotten used to me.

The fact that Amp wasn't much bigger than

3

a stick of butter helped me keep him a secret from my parents and little brother. He also had an invisibility trick that came in handy more than once and the ability to erase people's short-term memory.

The only other person on Earth who knew about Amp was my best friend and next-door neighbor, Olivia. And she had gotten so used to Amp that it was a minor miracle she hadn't blurted out some funny story about him to my parents.

As the ambassador of the human race, I think I had done a pretty spectacular job. My cat hadn't eaten Amp, I hadn't stepped on him, and most important of all, I'd convinced him that attacking our planet was a bad idea.

See, Amp is the lead scout for the planet Erde. The Erdians are planning on taking over Earth, but because of me, Amp understood that attacking this planet was a major mistake. Compared to the average Erdian, we were simply too big to be defeated.

So, as we made slow progress in repairing his ship, the *Dingle*, we became friends—if it's possible for a human to be friends with a hairless, three-fingered, Smurf-colored alien.

But now the time was fast approaching to get Amp back home to cancel the Erdian invasion. The future of Earth and Erde depended on us. We both knew it, but we didn't talk about it much.

Mostly, we spent our time eating junk food and watching scary movies on my mom's laptop.

Amp was crazy for horror movies, the old black-and-white kind. *Dracula. Frankenstein. The Wolf Man. Creature from the Black Lagoon.* We were working our way through a deluxe set of twenty-four classic horror movies on DVD that I had borrowed from Olivia's grandpa.

One night, Amp and I were up late—as usual—enjoying SweeTarts and Ritz Crackers while watching *The Mummy* (starring Boris Karloff), when our cozy little situation got crazy.

As is often the case, it all started with alarm bells.

Sound the Alarm

"**H**ey, what's that noise?"

"Eh?" Amp grunted absent-mindedly. He was lying on his side next to the track pad on my mom's laptop, rubbing his stuffed belly, totally absorbed in the movie.

I was sitting cross-legged on my bed with the computer in front of me.

"Hey," I said, gently poking the back of his head with my pinky finger. "Can you hear that?"

"I can hear you interrupting the movie," he said. "Now shush."

"Seriously," I said, poking his shoulder now.

"Knock it off, Zack," he said, shrugging his poked shoulder.

"C'mon, Amp, listen."

"Quiet!" he said, waving his hand at me. "The

mummy is coming. I love this part!"

I slapped the space bar and paused the movie. "What are you—?"

"Can you hear it now?"

We both listened in the silence. It was a far-away tinkling, buzzing sound. Or beeping. It wasn't the kind of sound I had ever heard before.

"That sounds pretty dang alien to me," I whispered.

He jumped to his feet and held up his hands to silence me as he strained to hear the noise.

"Oh, that's not good," he said in his strange, high-pitched voice.

"What exactly do you mean by 'not good'?"

"Does it mean more than one thing?" he asked.

"Amp, what's happening?"

He began looking around in a panic. His face turned a paler shade of blue.

"Is that sound coming from you? Are you going to explode or something?"

He shot me a look. "Don't be ridiculous. I don't beep. Or explode."

"At first I thought you were farting," I half-joked, but it wasn't funny. The far-off beeping alarm grew louder.

"It's an Erdian alarm."

"Seriously?" I yelped, jumping off my bed. I dropped down to the floor and looked under the bed. I looked in my laundry basket. I opened all the drawers of my desk as fast as I could, but I seemed to get no closer to the sound. I noticed he was still standing on the laptop. "Are you just going to stand there?" I snapped.

"You can search faster than me," he said.

"Is the thing I'm looking for going to blow up in my face when I find it?!"

"Why do you always assume things are going to blow up?"

"That's the kind of noise things that blow up make!"

"Try the window," he said, pointing urgently.

I pulled up my window and looked out to the dark backyard. "Crickets," I said. "Only crickets outside. No alarm."

When I turned back around Amp was staring at the closet with a horrified expression on his face. We kept his spaceship in my closet!

Amp and I exchanged a glance.

I tiptoed over to my closet door, opened it

slowly, and gently pulled the wool blanket off his football-size spaceship. The alarm become louder as it fell away, and I noticed two small blinking purple lights.

My mind spun. "Do you need to change the oil or something?"

Amp appeared next to my foot. He grabbed the ample skin of his belly and began to nervously knead it like bread dough. "That is a proximity alarm," Amp said in a trembly, tight voice.

"That's terrible," I whispered, staring at the blinking light. "What exactly does *proximity* mean?"

"It means someone is coming," he said.

Party Crasher

"What do you mean, somebody is coming?" I asked.

Amp pulled on his antennas. "What do you think I mean? I mean what it sounds like I mean!"

I picked him up and held him just inches from my nose. "Don't get tricky, Short Pants."

"I don't wear pants! You know that."

"Don't get snarky, either. Just tell me what's happening."

He released his antennas, closed his eyes, and pulled down his lower lip. "I don't know."

"They're attacking Earth, aren't they?" I yelped, shaking him.

"Who is?"

"Your creepy Erdian friends! They're arriving

on Earth right now. The invasion is beginning, and I never warned anybody!"

"Whoa, whoa, whoa!" he wheezed, struggling in my grip. "Not so fast."

"Was this whole thing a trick? Were you just stalling? Faking me out about your broken ship until your army of blue buddies arrived?"

He pushed on my fingers. "You're squeezing me too tight," he gasped. "My head is going to pop!"

"Sorry," I said and opened up my hand. He took several deep breaths and began to pace in circles on my palm, just inches from my face.

"That, Zack, is not an invasion alarm," he said, pointing at his ship. "Invasion alarms are yellow."

"Why yellow?"

"It would take too long to explain," he said, waving off my question. "The point is that alarm just means that someone is coming."

"Someone? Or a million Erdian someones?"

He stared at the buzzing, flashing light and it stopped suddenly. He looked back at me. "They're probably trying to find me. Like a rescue mission of some kind. But because my ship is damaged, they'll never actually find me. The odds are a million to one."

I looked at him skeptically. "Who would they send? Your mom?"

"Why on Erde would they send my mother? That would make no sense. Let's just hope it's not my—"

Amp was interrupted by a thunderous whooshing sound coming from my window.

"The attack is beginning!" I squealed.

I dropped Amp like a hot potato, jumped out of the closet, scrambled to my desk, and pressed my face to the window screen. I squinted as a fiery light lit up the backyard.

"Uh-oh," Amp gasped from somewhere behind me.

A spaceship just like Amp's was flying in circles twenty feet off the ground in our backyard. A shower of orange and white sparks were spraying out of it, making it look like the Fourth of July had come to my backyard.

Without warning, it turned sharply, like it had bounced off an invisible wall.

"Ooohhhhh nooooooo . . ."

I dove to the carpet just as the thing exploded through my window screen.

Just like Amp's ship had done, the fizzing ball of metal crashed into the wall over my bed with a dull thud, just two feet from the dent Amp's ship had made, which I had cleverly hidden from my family by covering it with a baseball poster.

I was definitely going to need another poster now.

I blinked as thick, stinging smoke filled my room. A burning rubber taste made my tongue tingle. And an eerie, glowing light pulsed from under my bed.

"A million to one, he says," I said, shaking my head in disbelief. Despite Amp's claim that the invasion wasn't starting, I wasn't convinced. He had been wrong before. About practically everything.

That's when I saw Amp crouching on my bedspread. He had put on his helmet and was holding his tiny weapon out in front of him. Like a truly good friend, he was trying to protect me.

Then he turned.

But then I realized that wasn't Amp on my bed.

It was another Erdian. And he looked ready for a fight.

04

My Second Erdian

"**R**eport to Erdian Council," the strange Erdian barked into a little wristband recorder thingy.

"Here we go again," I sighed, rising to my feet. I'd seen Amp do this a million times. This was like getting the same headache twice.

"Atmosphere on this planet is exactly as we predicted," he continued breathlessly into his tiny bracelet. "Readings indicate seventy-eight percent nitrogen, twenty-one percent oxygen, and trace amounts of argon and carbon dioxide. It is, however, having a strange effect on my voice, which sounds very high. No sign yet of

Scout First Class Amp. Stand by for more. Situation here is fluid and unpredictable."

Now that I had a better look at him, I did notice that this Erdian had slightly longer antennas than Amp and a big space in his teeth. Other than that, they were practically identical.

I cleared my throat. "Uh . . . hi, I'm Zack," I announced.

He spun and faced me. "Do not move, Earth person," the tiny creature commanded, his eyes growing wide with fear. He stumbled backward on my bedspread.

I knew he was surprised by my size.

When Amp had arrived so many weeks ago, he was surprised when he saw how big I was. And when he saw the size of my parents, he practically fainted.

I sighed as I stepped over to my bed. "Okay, just take it easy, squirt," I said. "I come in peace."

"You come in peace?" he said. "But I'm the one who just got here!"

Do all Erdians love to argue? "Listen, I am on

your side. Let's be friends."

"Oh, please, earthling, your weak mind tricks will not work on me."

"Mind tricks? Hey, I'm just being friendly."

"That won't work either," he said, pointing his little weapon at me, which looked like a tiny TV remote control.

"Whoa there, half-pint," I said. "Relax with the ol' remote-controller-zapper thingy. Look, I know the whole Erdian invasion backstory. So take it easy and tell me what you're doing here."

"You know about the invasion!" he cried. "You must have tortured our scout!"

"Tortured? Amp? C'mon, Blue Face, it's not like that."

He grunted at me. "He would have never revealed his name unless you forced him to. What have you done with his body? I am here to recover it."

"Body? He's not dead. Gosh, what do you think I am?"

"Then where is he? Huh? Tell me that, giant human!"

"Actually, I'm not sure. He's probably hiding somewhere. He can be like that."

"Oh, please, you expect me to believe that? You are a horrible liar!"

"Ease back on the throttle, space dude," I said soothingly. I tried to calm him down by flashing him with my friendliest, welcoming smile.

"Showing me your teeth will not scare me."

"That was a smi—! Oh, forget it! Look, we need to quiet down and clean up this mess before my parents come barging in here."

He crept closer to me. I'm sure he was trying to get me in range of his weapon. "Show me where you're keeping him prisoner this instant." His eyes nervously scanned the smoke-filled room. "Amp! Amp! I am here to rescue you!"

He then spoke in a strange language that I couldn't follow. It was Erdian. Amp had taught me a few words, but they were mostly curse words.

"Could you be quiet, please?" I hissed. "If my mom and dad hear you they'll flatten you with a spatula. You want to get pancaked?"

"AMP! AMP! IDENTIFY YOUR LOCATION!"

This guy had listening issues. "Stop with the floofy shouting."

I thought using an Erdian word like *floofy* would

make him feel at ease, but it only seemed to freak him out more.

"NOTHING IS AS IT SHOULD BE!" he yelped.

Without any other ideas, I half-fell, half-dove onto my bed in front of him.

That took my tiny visitor by complete surprise.

The resulting mattress bounce sent him flying high into the air, at least three feet. I counted four somersaults, one spin, and two and a half twists. I caught him gently in the palm of my hand.

Amp and I did this trick all the time. It was hilarious. But my new guest didn't seem to see the humor in it.

Shaking his head, he jumped to his feet and zapped my chin with his weapon. It felt like cold static electricity. It tickled. He snarled and shot me repeatedly in the lips, ears, eyes, forehead, cheeks, and nostrils. He seemed to be looking for a weak spot.

I rolled my eyes at him. Then I plucked his helmet off his head and put it on the tip of my nose. His stunned look made me laugh.

"Let's get one thing straight," I began.

Before I could finish, he was knocked from my hand by a flying marshmallow.

05

Marshmallow Bullets

"NO! WAIT!" I yelped.

One minute you're making intergalactic peace with an alien, and in the next second he's picked off by a flying marshmallow!

Another marshmallow came flying. This one bounced off the back of my head. It stung more than I'd care to admit.

Olivia!

One of Olivia's many charming hobbies is building marshmallow launchers. Or, in this case, marshmallow cannons.

I looked back over my shoulder just as a spinning marshmallow rocketed through the ragged hole in my screen. It hit me square in the eye.

"Agh!" I said, falling back on my bed. "Olivia, knock it off," I said in the loudest whisper I could muster.

When I spun back around the strange Erdian was gone.

"This can't be happening," I said.

Marshmallows continued to fly past my head. One hit me square in the ear. My best friend and next-door neighbor could be annoying, but there was no denying she had great aim.

I stepped to the window. "Olivia, what are you—"

Three marshmallows bounced off my face in less than two seconds. "OUCH!"

"Sorry," I heard her call out.

I could see Olivia's shadowy figure standing barefoot in the grass in my backyard. She was in a nightgown and carrying her largest marshmallow launcher. It was slung over her shoulder by a guitar strap.

"That thing is dangerous, Olivia." I sniffed, trying to clear my watery eye.

"Oh my gosh, Zack, are you crying?"

I growled. "You almost blinded me! What are you doing?" I hissed, poking my head all the way out of my screen's new basketball-size hole.

"I'm running outta ammo, that's what I'm doing!" she said. "Duh, Zack. I'm laying down a steady suppressing fire so you can safely retreat."

"Retreat? Where am I going to retreat to? I'm already in my room!"

"You can't argue with basic military tactics, Zack."

"Did you see the—"

"Of course," she interrupted. "I think the whole neighborhood did. It sounded like World War III out here. What's going on?!"

"I have no idea. Hopefully it's not going to start raining Erdians in a few seconds."

"WHAT?! We need a plan!"

"Hold on!"

One thing I had to admit about Olivia, she was clear-thinking in an emergency. I, on the other hand, had a brain that turned into pink yogurt when things got tense.

I turned back to my room. I waved away the smoke that hung in the air. I couldn't see movement anywhere. Just as I was about to call out his name, I saw Amp by the door. He was jumping up and down and waving his arms.

At that moment, he sent me one of his brain balls. He could toss thoughts right into my head.

"We must leave now!" he yelped inside my mind. "GET ME OUTTA HERE!"

Without another word, I reached him in four big hops, snatched him up off the carpet, and slipped out my bedroom door.

I looked down the dark hallway. The coast

27

seemed clear. I gave Amp a look, but it was too dark to see his face. I stuffed him headfirst into my shirt pocket.

I zipped down the upstairs hallway, avoiding the creaky spots, crept down the stairs, and slipped out the back door.

I stood on our backyard patio, feeling the cold concrete under my bare feet, and let out a big sigh.

"Don't move," a voice hissed just inches from my ear.

I felt the barrel of a marshmallow launcher on my lower back.

Olivia.

"Are you crazy? I almost karate chopped you in the face," I whispered.

Amp cleared his throat. "Uh, Zack, I think I just threw up a little bit in your pocket."

"Oh, that is just so gross," Olivia whispered.

"Just when you think a night can't get any weirder," I grumbled.

Retreat and Rethink

"**H**as the Erdian invasion started, or what?" Olivia grunted as she climbed through her bedroom window.

"Amp says no, but when was the last time he was right about anything," I said, standing just outside her window.

"You know I can hear you, right?" Amp said from my pocket.

I quickly scanned the starry sky once more for Erdian spaceships. I saw nothing. "Seriously? Half the time you don't know what you're talking about."

"I beg your pardon," Amp called out from my pocket. "I object to that. I'm telling you that it's not the invasion. The timing is all wrong."

"Says the guy who recently stole my bike's

brakes and ended up breaking my arm," I said.

"You didn't break it," Olivia corrected from inside. "You separated your shoulder."

I hoisted myself up onto Olivia's window-sill. "Whatever! Amp said they'd never find him. A-million-to-one odds, he assured me."

"I don't remember saying that," Amp mumbled.

"And now you've barfed in my pocket. It's starting to feel moist in there. Could anything be grosser than alien puke?"

"What if you're wrong about the invasion, Amp?" Olivia asked, jumping from her desk to her bed. "We're going to need a lot more firepower than a single homemade marshmallow launcher."

"I don't know," I said, "that thing seems pretty deadly."

A minute ago we had slipped through the loose plank in the fence between our two back-yards, but the side door to her garage was locked. Her dusty, crowded garage was where we usually chatted about things like the survival of the human race and preventing alien invasions. Now, with nowhere else to go, we retreated through her bedroom window.

Thankfully it was on the first floor.

"It is not an invasion," Amp grumbled from my shirt pocket as I stepped onto Olivia's desk, which sat conveniently just under her window. "Remember, that light was purple, not yellow."

"What light?" Olivia asked.

Amp popped up from my pocket and grumpily waved off Olivia's question. He smacked his lips. "Does anyone have a mint? I have vomit breath."

Olivia rolled her eyes. She began reloading her marshmallow launcher with a giant bag of marsh-mallows she apparently kept under her bed for just such an occasion. "Mind getting down, Zack? You're standing on my book report."

"We have a book report due?" I whispered, lifting up my left foot.

"It's not due until next week," she said.

"And you're already done? Boy, this night just keeps getting stranger."

Olivia and I are in the same class at school, but when it comes to homework, Olivia is in a class all her own.

"We need to do something pronto, guys," Olivia said, now sitting on her unmade bed, fully-loaded marshmallow launcher in her lap. "Amp, who was in that rocket ship?"

"His name is Ohm," Amp said.

"He's a very tense Erdian guy who looks just like Amp," I said, climbing carefully down from Olivia's desk and sitting in her chair. "They're twins."

"What?" Amp said, kicking me through my shirt. "Ohm looks nothing like me! I'm quite handsome compared to him."

"Really? You look like clones," I said, plucking him from my pocket and placing him gently on Olivia's book report.

"It doesn't matter what he looks like," Olivia said. "Zacky, there's a strange alien wandering around your house."

"I shut my door," I said quietly.

"We have to go talk to him," Olivia announced, standing up.

Amp groaned and looked at the ceiling. "I just wanted to finish my movie."

"We're not going anywhere until Amp tells us who that guy is," I said.

"He's the last person I wanted to see," Amp groaned.

"Is he your dad?"

"My dad? Of course not!"

"Your cousin?"

"No."

"Uncle? Sister? Brother? Dance instructor?"

"No. No. No. And no."

"Is he your favorite Erdian movie star?" Olivia asked, with a hopeful smile.

"WHAT? No! That's ridiculous. Please stop guessing. My head is starting to hurt. Ohm is not my cousin, uncle, or dance instructor." Amp sighed. "He's like your PE teacher at school, but bossier, louder, and stricter."

"You've seen Ms. Lutter," Olivia scoffed. "There's no way any Erdian is worse than her!"

Amp's tiny shoulder slumped in defeat. He pulled down on his antennas. He sighed heavily. "Let's see, I'm trying to think of the right word in English. I guess you could call Ohm my boss, or trainer, or the captain of my team of scouts."

"So," Olivia said, summarizing, "your drill sergeant, Mr. Ohm, has shown up to kick your mini booty all over the Earth for screwing up your mission."

Amp groaned nervously. "He's gonna scream into my antennas all night long."

"But hold on," I said. "What if Amp's wrong? What if this Ohm character is just the first Erdian to show up? There could be Erdians dancing in the streets in a few minutes."

"Why would they be dancing?" Amp asked, shaking his head in confusion.

"Zack's right, Ampy, we can't stay over here hiding," Olivia said. "We need to figure out what this Ohm is up to."

"And I have to make sure he doesn't leave my room and get turned into a chew toy by Mr. Jinxy," I said, standing.

Amp looked miserable, like he was about to cry. "I guess you're right. But could you at least leave your food bazooka here? It sends the wrong message."

Olivia looked down at her marshmallow blaster. She shrugged and tossed it on her bed. I flinched, thinking it might accidentally fire off another round.

"Hurry," I said. "I can't have my mom finding an alien in my room. She won't even let me have a tortoise."

Amp sighed before he disappeared into my pocket, looking more a shade of gray than blue.

07

Sugar Bust

We crept silently through the back door of my dark house, down the silent hallway, and halfway up the stairs when my mom called out my name from the kitchen.

"Zackary Frederick McGee, get in here."

Olivia and I froze.

Calling me by my full name was never a good sign.

It must have been well after midnight by now and well past visiting hours.

Olivia grabbed my wrist and squeezed it. "What is she doing up?" she whispered. Her face was just inches from mine, but it was so dark on the stairs I couldn't see her expression.

"Wait here," I said. I pulled Amp from my pocket and placed him in her hand. I took a deep breath and made my way into the dim kitchen, which was lit only by the small light above the stove. Mom was sitting at the table with her back to me.

"Hey, Mom, what are you doing up?" I said as casually as I could.

"I could ask the same of you," she said coldly, not turning around. "Sit down, Zack."

A million thoughts raced through my mind. Did she know Olivia was standing on the stairs? Or that she was holding a squirming alien? Or, even worse, could she have walked in on Ohm and been zapped repeatedly?

I had no idea what she knew, so I decided to play dumb, which, sadly, comes pretty naturally to me.

"What's up?" I said, flopping into the chair opposite her.

That's when I saw something that made me accidentally squeak in panic. Piled high on the table in front of my mom was a mountain of marshmallows, at least fifty of them. And scattered throughout this spongy pyramid of sugary goodness were a few dozen SweeTart wrappers and half-eaten rolls of Ritz Crackers.

My mind spun, but I couldn't think of anything to say.

"Not only are you sneaking around in the middle of the night, your room is covered with marshmallows. I stepped on them when I went in there. Pretty gross, Zack."

"You went in my room?" I yelped.

"You're sneaking food into your room."

"Those marshmallows are not technically mine."

"They're everywhere, Zack. And I found the hole in your window screen. Is that how you're sneaking in all this junk food?"

"What? No! That hole is . . . well, yes, the marshmallows did come through that hole, but it's—"

"And these candy wrappers?"

"Those aren't mine either, you know, like, legally." Even as I said it I thought I sounded ridiculous.

"And then there's that smell."

"Smell?"

"I smelled smoke in there, young man."

"Smoke? Really?"

"A burning smell."

"Well, doesn't most smoke have a burning smell?"

"Don't get smart with me."

Smart? I was playing dumb. I tried my best to look confused. "I have no idea what smell you're talking about."

"Are you cooking eggs in your room?"

"Eggs? What? Seriously, Mom? Do you think I'm running a truck stop in there?"

"Maybe! You tell me, Zack. I was overcome with the smell of rotten eggs in my own son's room." Her eyes got watery, either from emotion or the act of recalling the smelly egg smell. "I actually gagged—in my own house!" she continued. "Cooking eggs in your room? That is not safe. You're putting your whole family in danger."

"What? I was not cooking eggs. Trust me. It's probably just my baseball cleats under my bed or something, covered with some kind of sock mold or toe fungus."

I instantly knew what the smell really was. It was Ohm, making my mom think she was smelling rotten eggs. It was an Erdian mind trick, not unlike a skunk's defense, but you only think you're smelling something disgusting. Amp had done this trick to me before.

The terrible smell was overwhelming, and a great way to get rid of someone. But it was also something I could not easily explain to Mom without blowing the whole aliens-are-in-your-house-right-now thing.

I squirmed in my chair. At least it sounded like she hadn't seen the new dent in the wall above my bed. That was something to be thankful for.

"And there's a big dent in your wall," she said. "I can't imagine what that is from."

"I think Olivia did that," I muttered. Talk about throwing your best friend under the bus. I could swear I heard Olivia grunt in protest outside the kitchen.

Mom stared at me with a mixture of anger, puzzlement, and disappointment—the big three. "I'm calling my sister tomorrow. Your aunt Joni is a dietician and she can help you see the error of your ways."

"Most of that isn't even mine," I protested, staring at the mountain of empty calories in front of me.

She shook her head at me. "Marshmallows? SweeTarts? Ritz Crackers? Rotten eggs? I'm speechless, Zack!"

"Speechless? Oh, you seem to be doing okay."

She narrowed her eyes at me. "Watch your tongue, Willy Wonka. I don't want to find any more wrappers or walk in on you roasting marshmallows.

Or cooking a Denver omelet. Got it?"

I wanted to argue, but couldn't stop thinking about the strange alien up in my room and the possibility that we were just minutes from a global invasion.

And I couldn't explain a single thing without blowing Amp's cover, or think fast enough to come up with a half-good lie.

That's when I saw Olivia poking her head in the kitchen doorway right over my mom's shoulder. She was waving at me to come urgently. Her teeth were clenched. Her eyes were bugged out.

What now?

I did a fake yawn and said I was sorry. I got up, gave Mom a half-hearted sideways hug, and told her I'd clean up the mess in my room. "Don't worry, my diet isn't as bad as it looks."

She didn't hug me back, which was good, because if she had, she might have seen Olivia waving like a lunatic just a few feet behind her.

Bedspread Rumble

"**W**hat were you going on about in there?" Olivia hissed. "Like two old ladies having tea and crumpets!"

"What the heck is a crumpet?"

"We've kind of got an urgent situation here, Zack."

I sighed. "She thinks I've got a junk-food-eating problem."

"She's right about that."

"Thanks for your support."

From around the corner, I could hear my mom throwing away the mountain of marshmallows and crinkly old candy wrappers.

"So, Amp, how do you want to play this?" I asked into the darkness.

"Amp's not here right now," Olivia said. "He

bit me on the finger—the rat—and then he ran off."

"Are you serious? Maybe he really is in cahoots with this Ohm guy. Maybe they're working together. I don't know what's going on. Which way did he go?"

"I don't know. I forgot my night vision goggles."

"I didn't know you had night vision goggles."

She was silent and still for a moment. "I was joking," she said flatly.

"Well, he could be anywhere by now. He could be up on the roof directing the Erdian traffic."

Just then, Olivia and I both flinched.

"HELP! THIS! GOT! EYE! GLECH!" Amp shouted inside my head. It was a brain ball tossed directly into my skull from wherever he was. The gasped words seemed to echo in my brain as they slowly faded away.

"Whoa. Did he brain-whisper to you, too?" Olivia asked.

"Yes, I hate when he does that! It's like wearing someone else's pants."

"It sounded like he's choking on a pretzel."

"Maybe Mr. Jinxy is chewing on his tiny head right now."

The light above the stove snapped off in the kitchen. My mom would be heading up these stairs in seconds. "C'mon," I whispered, pulling Olivia by the pajama sleeve.

I could hear the shuffling of my mom's slippers as we made it to the top of the stairs. We tiptoed down the hall, opened my door as silently as possible, and slipped into my room.

There we were met with a sight so shocking and odd that neither of us moved a muscle.

Amp and Ohm were squared off in front of each other on my rumpled bedspread. They appeared to be in the middle of a fight, but they weren't touching each other—but they were fighting just the same!

Amp grabbed at his throat. Ohm was body-slammed. Suddenly, Amp's legs were kicked out from under him and he fell onto his back, wriggling in pain. Ohm then floated five inches into the air and was driven downward onto the top of his head. Amp then clutched his eyes and stumbled around blindly. All these crazy movements were accompanied by a wild assortment of grunts, growls, yelps, howls, and Erdian words, which I can only assume were naughty.

Olivia and I watched the bizarre match in silence as each Erdian inflicted invisible blows on the other.

"It's like shadow boxing, but the shadow

actually makes contact," Olivia said.

We watched as Amp stuffed a fist in his own mouth and gagged. Ohm yelped loudly and began hopping in circles as his little leg was bent painfully back behind him.

"They're fighting with their minds," I said. "That's the dumbest thing I've ever seen. Or maybe this is how Erdians say hello. A mental handshake that looks like cage fighting."

"No, I'm pretty sure they're hurting each other," Olivia said.

Before I could stop her, she picked up the glass of water I kept next to my bed and splashed the two stumbling and grunting combatants.

The cold water had the intended effect: the two Erdians were soaked out of their mental battle. They stood there, dripping on the giant wet spot that now stained my bedspread.

"Hey, that's where I sleep!" I protested, but Olivia wasn't listening.

"You two are hundreds of years old, but you're acting like children," Olivia scolded. "I will put you both in a pickle jar for a month if you don't shake hands right now."

Boy, Olivia seemed ready to get into the scuffle herself if these two didn't make friends fast.

"Why on . . . Erde would we . . . shake our hands?" Ohm said, gasping for air.

"Yes, that makes no sense," Amp agreed, not taking his eyes off Ohm.

"Just do it," I said. "You don't want to tangle with Olivia when she's mad, trust me."

"Now shake hands and make up," Olivia growled, staring the two down.

Still not taking their eyes of each other, the two huffing and puffing Erdians both raised their three-fingered hands into the air and began shaking them, like a silent cheer at a basketball game.

Olivia turned her head toward me and slowly shook her head. I think she was holding back a smirk. "Look, Zack, they're shaking hands."

"They sure are," I said with a smile. "Now that's more like it."

09

The Inspection

Since the Erdians were momentarily at peace in my room, and Olivia was technically my visitor, I decided to take the lead in questioning the strange Erdian.

"Listen, Mr. Ohm, what are you doing here? Is the invasion starting or what?"

"You told them?" he barked at Amp.

I snapped my fingers to get Ohm's attention again. "Hey, you obviously didn't travel through those wormholes that go through space like Swiss cheese just to fight an imaginary wrestling match with my Erdian houseguest."

Apparently, Ohm was not impressed with my knowledge of space travel, which was easy to see by the way he scrunched up his face. "Don't they learn about science on this planet?" he asked Amp.

"They do," Amp replied with a shrug. "Some are better at it . . . than others." He said this while gesturing to Olivia and then to me when he said "others."

"Oh, stuff it," I said. "You can't even fix your own spaceship, smarty-pants."

"What?" Ohm exclaimed, turning again to Amp. "What's wrong with your vehicle?"

"That's what I've been trying to tell you. I've spent my time here repairing my ship," Amp said.

"And destroying my perfectly ordinary childhood in the process," I grumbled.

Olivia harrumphed in frustration. "Uh, could we get back to the more pressing issue of whether we're being invaded by little green men from outer space?"

"Blue, you mean," Amp corrected, looking down as if to double-check his color.

Ohm just waved Olivia away like a fly at a picnic. "Attention, Scout Amp!" Ohm barked. Amp snapped instantly into a tall, rigid stance, fists at his side, antennas straight up, eyes staring straight ahead.

Olivia and I looked at each other in surprise.

Ohm looked Amp up and down like he was inspecting a used car for sale. He walked slowly around him, shaking his head in disappointment. I could swear he made a "tsk-tsk" sound when he looked at Amp's backside.

When he reached his original position in front of Amp, he nodded and Amp seemed to collapse back into his natural slump, exhausted from the effort of standing at attention.

"What happened to you?" Ohm asked.

"The atmosphere damaged my ship's central—"

"I'm not talking about your ship; I'm talking about you. Look at you! It looks like you've eaten a lifetime's supply of gribble grubs."

Olivia and I looked at each other. "Gribble grubs? Seriously?" she said.

"It is true," Amp said, looking down at his feet, "I have grown fond of the earthling's food."

"He can go through a roll of SweeTarts like a termite can go through a toothpick," I said, trying to help, but Amp shot me his please-shut-up look.

Ohm continued. "I thought you had a copilot behind you, but it just turns out to be your rear end."

"Oh, snap." Olivia giggled. Now it was my turn to shoot her a look.

"Where is your fight, solider? You're spilling Erdian secrets to these earthling spies like a Yommer's geyser."

"A what?" Olivia said, starting to enjoy herself.

"Hey, we're not spies!" I protested. "This is my

room. If anything, you're the spy!"

Olivia laughed and nodded at Ohm. "Oh, Zack got you good there, Grumpy Gills!"

Ohm didn't miss a beat. "You've grown pudgy and plump around the middle, scout. Distracted. Soft. Weak. Have you forgotten your mission? Your obligation to your fellow Erdian soldiers?"

"My ship was damaged!" Amp roared. "My communication system will not work from here! What was I to do?"

That was all I could stand. I shot my hand out and grabbed Amp's bossy boss and held him up in front of my face.

"Okay, yes, Amp's put on a couple of ounces," I said, "but he tried his hardest to warn everyone back on Erde not to come here."

Ohm thought about that one. He seemed to look at me carefully for the first time. "I saw a bigger version of you earlier. Huge."

"That was my mom. And don't call her huge, she wouldn't like it. She's just an adult. Most people are adults. And if you think she's big, you should see my dad. Heck, you should see my uncle Steve."

"It's true," Olivia said, nodding. "Zack's uncle Steve looks like a parade float."

I stared at Ohm. "We're too big for you Erdians. If you think you're going to take over this planet with your little zapper guns and rotten-egg mind tricks, you're in for a rude awakening."

"And you haven't even heard about cats yet." Olivia said. "There are millions of them, and they were built for hunting and eating Erdians. Mr. Jinxy is probably just outside Zack's door waiting for snack time."

Hearing our words, the Erdian in my fist sagged a bit. He seemed to be thinking about what I said. He looked at me, then Olivia, then back at me. "Yes, perhaps you're right. We have miscalculated. Amp and I must return immediately to cancel this attack."

"Now that's more like it," Olivia said.

Ohm looked at the device on his wrist and pressed a few buttons. "But we are almost out of time. Our next opportunity for optimum planet alignment is tomorrow night, when your moon is at perigee. We will both leave in my ship tomorrow night."

"Erdian Council note. It seems that the young earthlings are unaware that their only moon orbits around their planet in an irregular oval shape, including a point when the moon is closest to their planet-called perigee-and a point when it's farthest from Earth-called apogee."

Amp and I looked at each other, ignoring Ohm's lesson on moon orbits.

Tomorrow would be our last day together.

Chatty Bang-Bang

Olivia left shortly after we decided on a launch the next night in my backyard.

Trouble was, tomorrow was Saturday. My mom, dad, and nosy little brother would be around all day. And I was afraid my secret would get exposed before we could send the Erdian scouts on their way.

Of course, the idea of Amp leaving tomorrow impacted me more than I might have imagined. I always knew this time would come, but the thought of never seeing Amp again after tomorrow night choked me up.

The odds of me coming to visit him on Erde were somewhere between never and not gonna happen. I thought I'd feel thrilled when he left, but I felt more like I'd been punched in the gut.

I was going to miss him.

Amp and Ohm were sitting on the small table next to my bed in the glow of my alarm clock, where they had been chatting away for the last hour. They were each sitting on leftover marshmallows from Olivia's launcher, which turned out to be the perfect size for Erdian chairs.

"Listen, you two, can you stop your gabbing? You're keeping me awake. I feel like I have sawdust in my eyes."

The Erdians stopped blabbing in their alien language and considered me for a moment. Ohm—at least I think it was Ohm—spoke into his wrist device.

> "Note to Erdian Council. Apparently humans must stop using their thinking organ during this planet's dark period. Further study required to determine how their brains become damaged while thinking, and what process restores them to full functionality."

Amp cleared his throat, then added a report of his own.

> "Council note. Human boy claims to have things called dreams while his brain is repairing itself. I believe these are random thoughts generated by an unoccupied mind. Curiously, subject reports he often dreams of eating a salami sandwich full of worms while wearing only his underwear in front of his classmates."

I rubbed my temples. I was being annoyed in stereo.

"What is an underwear?" Ohm asked quietly.

I grunted in the darkness. "Do you mind, Amp? That dream was private. It was supposed to be between you and me."

"No, you said I had to promise to never tell another living human being," he said, and pointed to Ohm. "Does he look human to you?"

"I seriously can't wait till you guys are no longer on my planet," I said. I folded my pillow around my head so as to block out their squeaky voices and pulled my knees up to my chin to avoid the water spot Olivia had made earlier to break up the Erdian fight.

Thankfully, I fell asleep shortly after telling the aliens to pipe down.

I dreamed of a wormy salami sandwich again, which I was eating in my boxers while standing in front of my stunned classmates. I wish I knew what this dream meant. I don't even like salami. Or worms. Or boxers.

In the morning, the Erdians were nowhere to be seen. I showered and made my way downstairs.

My stomach was already setting off four-alarm hunger pangs. I could hear my family talking quietly at the breakfast table.

It got quiet when I walked in. Mom, Dad, and Taylor watched me come in and flop down in my usual seat. They met me with blank stares. Nobody moved.

"What?" I said.

They all exchanged silent looks.

My mom cleared her throat. "Darling, it looks like you wet the bed. Taylor showed me the spot."

"That's from a glass of water," I said. "You didn't see anything weird in there, did you?"

"How much weirder does it get?" Taylor asked.

"You shouldn't drink such a big glass before you go to bed," Dad said, with a sad smile.

"No, you guys don't get it. Olivia did that."

Mom looked over at Dad, concern washing over her face.

"You have to stop blaming Olivia for everything," Mom said sternly. "Did Olivia make you drink that water before going to bed?"

I held my head in my hands. "No. You guys don't get it."

"Perhaps all those marshmallows made him thirsty," Taylor said, making a face at me.

At that moment, Mom slid a small plate of mini carrots, a scrambled egg white, and half a piece of dry wheat toast over in front me. "Let's start the day off eating right," she said with a look of pity. "Aunt Joni suggested this for your breakfast."

"Zack's on a special diet?" Taylor asked, delighted at my misery. "Is it because he's getting chunky? Or because he's wetting the bed now?"

At that very moment, I wanted to tell them everything.

I really did.

I wanted to run upstairs, find those chatty

aliens, and drop them into the pitcher of orange juice at the center of the kitchen table. I was so tired of keeping secrets. Of getting blamed for everything, when I was just trying to save the world. It was just too much for one kid to take!

I took a deep breath. One more day. I just had to get through one more day.

Then it'd all be over.

I would tell them all about it once it was over. But not now—we were so close! I couldn't blow Amp's cover now. Everything would be ruined. The Erdians would be carted off to some government research facility and be dissected like frogs. My house would probably become a museum.

I would have to find some way to push through the unfairness of it all.

I looked at each member of my family and started eating my carrots in crunchy silence.

They went back to eating.

While I secretly fed my egg whites to Smokey under the table, it occurred to me that our faithful dog was the one member of my family who seemed to offer any help to a kid under a lot of stress.

11

Healthful to a Fault

"**C**andy like SweeTarts is okay once in a while, for a special treat," my aunt Joni told me patiently. "But the natural sugars found in bananas, apples, and oranges are a more healthful option."

"Is *healthful* even a word?" I muttered.

Aunt Joni and I were in my living room. She had brought a variety of colorful posters showing different food groups and whatnot, which were perched on four folding tripods she must have used at her job. She was a nurse and dietician who worked at the local hospital. My mom had asked her to come over and set me straight on the basics of healthy eating.

This was no way to spend a perfectly good Saturday afternoon.

Learning about protein and the three different kinds of fat was shockingly boring. It was worse than school, and I thought nothing could be duller than school.

Here it was my last day ever with Amp, and I was stuck fidgeting on our rarely used fancy couch. I didn't want to be rude to my aunt, but I was having trouble paying attention. I desperately needed a plan for launching Ohm's spaceship, so the invasion of my planet could finally be canceled—but here I sat!

There was so much to say to Amp. So many things I needed to know about what was out there. If nothing else, at least we could have finished watching *The Mummy*. He loved that movie.

About an hour into Aunt Joni's lecture, I started drooling from boredom. My left leg fell asleep twice. My stomach growled like a wounded animal.

"Now here are some examples of healthful foods a young baseball player should know about."

If she said the word *healthful* one more time, I thought I might start weeping.

That's when I realized I wasn't alone on the couch.

Movement to my right caught my eye. I looked

down to see Amp and Ohm reclining comfortably, just inches from me, listening intently to my aunt drone on.

"How long have you been here?" I blurted out.

My aunt Joni looked surprised by my outburst. "Only two hours, sweetie. I should be done in about forty minutes."

I was still not used to the fact that Erdians could make themselves invisible. They did this with one of their Jedi mind tricks. Amp had explained once that he wasn't actually invisible; instead he just made the person instantly forget that they were seeing him at the same time they were seeing him.

See, it's hard to think about invisibility, let alone explain it!

"Is everything all right?" Aunt Joni asked, tapping her little pointer thing on her poster to redirect my attention.

"Be quiet," Amp said inside my head. I tried to shake off his brain ball, which now echoed in my head. "We're actually enjoying this presentation. This is truly fascinating."

"Could you please shut up?" I whispered, pressing my palms on my ears.

"I beg your pardon," my aunt said, lowering her pointer.

"No, not you," I said to her.

"We need to talk to you, human," Ohm said too loudly inside my head. "We have a problem with the launch."

"Could you please zip it for a minute," I growled. "My brain is going to explode."

"I can speak slower if you want," my aunt said, confused.

Without any warning, our cat, Mr. Jinxy, suddenly leaped onto the coffee table in front of me. He seemed to appear out of nowhere. His eyes were focused like laser beams on the two delicious aliens sitting next to me. I watched in horror as he lowered his head and crouched into an attack position.

Erdian invisibility tricks don't work on cats.

Both Erdians shot off down the couch. Mr. Jinxy catapulted out of his crouching-tiger position and gave chase.

All this happened so fast that I didn't have time to think. I went after the Erdians, thinking I could reach them faster than Mr. Jinxy if I took a better angle.

Unfortunately, the Erdians tried to use my aunt's tripods to cover their retreat, which didn't work on the darting Mr. Jinxy, but worked pretty well on me.

I heard my aunt scream as I scampered under her food displays on all fours, sending the tripods crashing and her posters falling in every possible direction. I can't be sure, but I think she whacked me on the back with her pointer, trying to get me back on the couch.

Luckily, I managed to block Mr. Jinxy with my shoulder and grab up an Erdian in each hand, a split second before Mr. Jinxy would have swatted

them into the carpet with his paw. He meowed in frustration, showing me his tiny, sharp fangs.

With my back turned, I stuffed the Erdians into my sweatshirt pockets, knowing that they may have forgotten to make themselves invisible to my aunt during all the excitement.

The chase could not have taken more the three seconds, but the living room was now a disaster. My aunt stared at me like I was a gorilla in a tuxedo. I smiled crookedly. Teary-eyed, she walked past me without saying another word, obviously eager to tell my mom that I was the rudest boy ever to walk this planet.

"Darn, I wanted to hear the rest of that," Amp said inside my head, "but I suppose we have more pressing matters."

"What now?" I sighed.

"Ohm's spaceship was damaged like mine," Amp said. "We need a new initial launch system, and we need it fast."

"Of course we do," I groaned.

12

Beard Boy

I was grounded.

Mom said I could not leave my room until I had grown a beard.

I think she was kidding.

But once she had seen Aunt Joni crying, somebody had to pay.

"This is Zack One, over," I said into my walkietalkie. "I repeat: this is Zack One. Come in, Twinkle Fairy Pants. Over."

"Twinkle Fairy Pants?" Amp squawked. "What on Erde is that?"

I dropped the walkie-talkie into my lap. "It's Olivia's new call sign. I know it's stupid, but she won't answer to anything else. I think she just likes to make me say it. Trust me, I feel like an idiot."

"Clever girl," Amp said to Ohm with a chuckle.

Ohm seemed to not get any of it. "Perhaps we could use this crude communication device to contact Erde—"

"No," I said, cutting him off. "We already tried that, to disastrous results."

I was sitting in my closet, both Erdian spaceships parked in front of me. The Erdians were between the ships, each sitting on a marshmallow. Amp had started nibbling on his seat every minute or so, and now a chunk of his marshmallow was missing.

"So now you like marshmallows?" I asked.

"Look, I'm an emotional eater," Amp exclaimed, repeating something he must have heard my mom say. "This whole situation is giving me the munchies."

"Munchies?" Ohm said, shrinking back in alarm. "Is that contagious?"

"Zack One," my walkie-talkie blurted out. "This is Twinkle Fairy Pants. Over."

"Where have you been?" I said, leaning into the microphone more than I needed. "We've got a problem with the boys and their car." I gave Ohm a wink or two, letting him know these were the secret code words we used when talking on the walkie-talkie.

"Is something stuck in his eye?" Ohm asked Amp, not getting the wink thing.

"I was helping my grandpa replace the condenser unit in the refrigerator, Wacky Zacky. What did those two blue bummers break now? Over."

Both Erdians looked offended. "Uh, the two bummers can hear you," I said, pressing the button. "Over."

"Oh, sorry, guys, no offense," Olivia said matter-of-factly through the tiny speaker. "We still blasting off at perigee?"

"Perigee?" I asked, confused.

"Perigee, dude," Olivia answered. "When the moon's orbit is closest to Earth. Those guys need to blast off at exactly one minute after midnight. I looked it up on the internet and worked out the timing."

Ohm looked surprised and impressed. "That timing is correct," he said.

I cleared my throat. "Uh . . . problem is that, just like Thing One's car, Thing Two's car can't get off the starting line."

The walkie-talkie was silent for a full thirty seconds. "Not again!" Olivia shot back, now sounding distressed.

"I know!" I said, eyeing the Erdians. "You'd think such an advanced civilization would have invented roadside towing service by now."

"We just need help getting high enough to fire off the secondary booster rockets," Amp

mumbled defensively. "We only have enough power for one boost."

"We already tried the rocket thing," Olivia said after a moment.

I shook my head at the memory. "We need something simpler this time. Something we can rig up in a few hours. Something that doesn't draw attention to itself. My house is crawling with unfriendlies."

The Erdians and I exchanged uneasy glances while we waited to hear back from the team member. Her voice eventually came back with no enthusiasm. "So we have no money. No time. No resources. Nobody to help us. It must be done in secret. And it has to work perfectly."

The Erdians looked at each other, then back at me, and nodded their heads in agreement.

"Yes, that about sums it up," I said, putting down the walkie-talkie.

I left the Erdians and my walkie-talkie in the dim light of my closet. I paced around my room and nervously pulled on my hair. Maybe tugging on my brain would spring loose a good idea.

It was already getting dark outside. The sun

was setting and we were no closer to coming up with a solution. I picked a few stale marshmallows off my carpet and ate them in silence.

That's when I spotted the great idea I had been looking for.

And it was right under my nose all this time!

13

Atlatl or Bust

"This is a tennis-ball-thrower thingy," I explained to the Erdians. "It helps you throw a ball farther. I use it when I take Smokey to the park."

"Is that the animal that tried to eat us?" Ohm asked, alarmed by the memory.

"No, that was Mr. Jinxy," I said. "Cats won't chase things you throw, only dogs."

"Why is that?" Ohm asked.

I shook my head in frustration. "I have no idea! You'd have to ask a cat. Look, just stay focused. See, we can use this ball thrower to launch your ship."

Both Erdians screwed up their faces in an odd way, like my idea gave them terrible gas.

They were both standing on my desk in front of me, each pulling down on their lower lip

skeptically. I could tell the Erdian twins weren't getting it.

"Here, watch," I said. I picked up a marshmallow and put it in the holder at the end of the ball thrower. With a grunt, I flung the ball chucker at the hole in my window screen. Both Erdians flinched, then spun and watched the white marshmallow rocket across our dark backyard and disappear over the fence near the garage.

"Whoa," they both said at the same time.

Excited now, I dropped to my knees and fished around under my bed for one of Smokey's chewed-up tennis balls. My hand found one and I placed it in the cup of the ball thrower.

I did the same thing with the tennis ball, but this time I got a running start and flung it even harder. It easily sailed over the roof of the garage.

"Impressive indeed," said one of the Erdians, I couldn't tell which.

I ducked down when a car alarm across the street started blaring. "Oops," I whispered giddily. "See, guys, this idea rocks."

I dropped the scuffed plastic thrower on the

desk and the Erdians began walking in circles around it, looking it up and down.

I was getting excited. "My dad says this thing is based on the atlatl, which was an Aztec weapon that combined the throwing device with a spear," I explained, enjoying teaching the Erdians a thing or two for a change.

"What does the word mean in the Aztec language?" Amp asked.

"Oh, atlatl?" I said, trying to remember. "I forget, but it was something like 'the thing that helps you throw things.'"

"Oh, I doubt that." Amp sniffed, giving me a disapproving look.

I shook my head. "It doesn't matter what it was called a million years ago."

"Probably humankind's first compound tool," Ohm said to Amp.

"Compound tool?" I said.

"*Compound* just means more than one part," Amp explained.

I cleared my throat, ready to make my case. "Yeah, well anyway, ancient humans made a device like this to throw spears or long darts when they were fighting or hunting. Apparently, atlatls were used for tens of thousands of years. They were eventually replaced by the bow and arrow, but that wasn't until fairly recently."

Amp considered me for a moment. "This clever idea uses the law of leverage to increase man's limited physical abilities."

"Limited?" I said. "I could flick you out the window with my pinky finger, Short Stuff."

"Exactly," Amp said. "But that's about it. Humans aren't very strong compared to other animals on Earth. You aren't quicker or tougher or bigger. You don't have long claws or big fangs. But humans are at the top of the food chain. Why is that?"

"Because we have brains?" I guessed. "Which we use to make compound tools? And things like the internet?"

"Exactly, Zack," Amp said, smiling with pride.

I noticed that Ohm was staring at me. "So you want to throw us into outer space with this plastic dog toy?"

"C'mon, you guys said you only have to get high enough for the secondary booster rockets, right? Ohm's spaceship is pretty light and no bigger than

a small football. I could tweak this a bit so it fits as snug as a bug in rug. You only need a good jump start, and I've got a strong arm! Everybody's afraid to steal second base on me."

Ohm pulled on his antennas and looked at Amp. "Snug bugs? Jump starts? Strong arms? Stolen bases? I cannot understand a word he says!"

"I still don't know what he's talking about half the time either," Amp replied quietly.

I sighed and sat on the corner of my bed. "This could work. Unless, of course, Olivia has come up with something better."

"Indeed," Amp said hopefully.

That's when I heard Olivia's ladder bump into the wall just outside my window.

14

Losing the Room

"**H**ello," Olivia called out from somewhere outside my second-story window. "Where are you guys?"

Her head now appeared and I saw her examine with some curiosity the hole in my screen.

"Shhh! Why didn't you just come to the front door?" I whispered.

"I did," she said, a little more quietly. "But your mom said you were grounded and I couldn't come back until you had grown a beard. What'd you do?"

"It's hard to explain," I said. "These guys almost became cat food."

She reached through the hole in the screen. "Here, put this on," she said, handing me a bulky plastic watch. "It's set to go off when we hit the launch window. It'll beep for one minute and

85

these guys have to take off during that minute, or it'll be too late. I have one, too," she said, holding up a smaller, sparkly pink watch that was now on her wrist.

I slipped on the heavy watch and then proceeded to tell Olivia all about my ball-thrower idea.

She was quiet for a few seconds. "You want to launch them into outer space with Smokey's ball thrower?" Olivia snickered, shaking her head. "That's the dumbest idea I ever heard."

"This crude mechanism might work," Ohm said without much enthusiasm. "Maybe."

Amp gave me a sideways glance and hopped up onto the ball thrower. "Actually, Olivia, this device uses the law of leverage to increase a human's throwing power. Kind of ingenious, for a primitive civilization."

"You seriously think this could work?" Olivia yelped, apparently jealous of my brilliance. "You've got to be kidding me, Amp!"

"Zack, demonstrate your throwing motion for Olivia," Amp said.

"Why?" I said.

"Just do it," Amp said. "If not for me, then for science."

I pretended to throw with the ball thrower, but I felt silly.

"Without the atlatl, you are limited by your size," Amp said. "The arc—or radius—you are able to make with your arm is actually quite small. But this atlatl device of yours increases the size of the radius your throwing motion makes."

"What's the size of my throwing radius have to do with anything?" I asked.

"The power your arm generates is constant," Ohm explained, "but by using a lever, you increase the velocity or speed of the ball, which increases the amount of kinetic energy you can generate, which makes the ball go farther."

Ohm said into his wrist device.

"Note to Erdian Council."

"Oh, please, not now," I begged, pressing a thumb on each of my temples.

"The law of the lever appears to be a foreign concept to these young earthlings. I will instruct: A lever is a movable bar that pivots on a fulcrum, like a seesaw. As a lever pivots on a fulcrum—which is the thing the lever is attached to—the points farther from the pivot move faster than parts closer to the pivot. If your elbow joint is the pivot in this case, and your arm the lever, holding this device will move the ball farther from the pivot, amplifying the force. Now do you understand?"

"I think my tiny brain just burst into flames," I said to Olivia.

She still seemed irritated by the simple brilliance of my idea. "No offense,

Zack, but this idea has epic failure written all over it."

"It does?" Ohm exclaimed, carefully examining the ball thrower. "Where?"

I rolled my eyes and grunted at Olivia. "Oh? And what have you come up with, Twinkle Fairy Pants?"

"I'm building a giant marshmallow launcher for Ohm's ship."

"Really?!" both Erdians shouted excitedly, clapping their tiny hands. "Let's see! Let's see!" they peeped like baby birds.

"What?" I yelped. "When? Have you even tested it?"

"C'mon, I'll show you guys," Olivia said, ignoring my questions. The Erdians jumped into her backpack. "You too, Zack."

I didn't budge.

"No thanks," I said stubbornly. "My idea rocks. I'm going to modify it for Ohm's ship, so it's ready when you guys come crawling back to me for help." I made a face at Olivia.

"Suit yourself," she said, sinking back down the ladder into the darkness. "We'll come get you

before the launch, which is now less than three hours away."

"Oh, you'll be back all right!" I called after them. "You'll see who's got the brains around here!"

15

Don't Move

My eyes flew open. I gasped. My room was dark.

The glowing numbers on my clock showed it was 11:57 p.m.!

I had fallen asleep—stupid wormy salami sandwich dream AGAIN!

"I did not mean to wake you," my Erdian friend said, startling me.

I turned my head on my pillow and it took a few seconds to realize it was Ohm standing on my chest, just inches from my chin. In the weak light, I could see him give me an unsteady, gap-toothed smile.

"I knew you guys would come crawling back!" I said, my heart starting to gallop. "I got an old tuna can out of the recycling and duct-taped it real good to the ball thrower! You should see it.

It's perfect! Your ship is in it and it's all ready to go. I think we should just—"

"Not so fast," Ohm said quietly. "We decided to go with Olivia's clever spring-loaded launcher. We took my ship while you were doing your dreams."

With a sense of dread, I realized I couldn't move a muscle. "Ugh," I grunted. It felt like a car was parked on top of me. "What did you do?" I said, panic rising in my voice. "Is this some kind of twisted Erdian mind trick?"

"This is for your own good," Ohm said, struggling to stay upright on my chest as I wriggled my body.

I peered down and could see that Ohm had tied me down to my bed. As my eyes focused, I saw that I was being held down by a crazy assortment of cords, shoestrings, dental floss, ribbons, bungee cords— even the belt from my bathrobe!

"You tied me down?" I growled, pulling at the two dozen restraints that now pinned me to my bed. "Dang it, Ohm, I need to say good-bye to Amp. It's our last chance to—"

"I don't want this departure to get messy. I could see how emotional you were about your atlatl idea.

Plus, it's obvious Amp has grown too attached to you. It's better this way. Less emotional. This is the Erdian way."

"The Erdian way is to tie a guy up? That is the dumbest thing I ever heard," I hissed at him. "This cannot be happening!"

That's when the alarm on the clunky plastic watch still strapped to my wrist started beeping.

"Oh no," I whispered.

"This is good-bye, I guess," said Ohm urgently. "I've got a flight to catch. Thank you for looking after my scout!"

I watched him make his way over to the window and jump out, disappearing into the darkness.

I was left alone, tied up, like a boat ready for a hurricane, watch beeping, tears building up in my eyes.

A movie Amp and I had watched several times flashed in my mind. It was an old black-and-white movie about the magician Harry Houdini and how he had become famous. I learned his fame wasn't the result of pulling rabbits out of a hat or making elephants disappear. He got famous by escaping from traps just like the one I was now in.

He was an escape artist.

So I just started doing what Houdini always did in the movie.

With all my might, I started flopping like a fish on the bottom of a boat, like bacon in a frying pan, like a guy who grabbed the end of a live wire. The beeping continued as I huffed and grunted and struggled like the great Houdini.

They made it look so easy in the movies!

But soon enough, my right leg freed itself and I started flopping and wriggling even harder. Soon both my legs were free, and I scooted myself down the bed until the rest of me escaped the assorted strings, belts, and cords holding me down!

I jumped off the bed and scrambled to my window, just in time to see Ohm's spaceship fly off Olivia's roof after a loud *CLACK* sound.

"NO!" I croaked.

Then I watched in horror as it turned end over end, making a lazy, soaring arc in the air. IT WASN'T HIGH ENOUGH! Not even close. It hit the tallest branch of a tree in my backyard and fell like a dead bird into the bushes near the fence.

I couldn't breathe.

"Epic fail," I whispered in shock.

The beeping continued.

There was still time!

I grabbed my modified ball chucker, clenched it in my teeth, and practically dove out my second-floor window.

I just hoped the ladder was still there.

16

Good-bye Forever

Luckily, the ladder was still under my window.

Unluckily, I fell off the ladder about halfway down.

I don't know how.

My foot just slipped and gravity did its thing.

I hit the ground like a basket of bricks and landed on my back on our wound-up garden hose, which helped cushion my fall, but the drop from that high up still knocked the wind out of me.

The beeping on my watch sounded louder.

I struggled like a turtle on its back to free myself from the hose and get to my feet.

The world seemed to spin under me.

My eyes were blurring with tears of emotion.

"Olivia," I whisper-yelled into the silence, into the darkness.

I stumbled my way across our dark backyard patio.

I caught sight of Olivia in the moonlight on the roof of her garage. She was waving her arms at me.

I heard a familiar voice in my head. "We are running out of time, earthling!"

"I'm coming! I'm coming!" I gulped, stumbling across the lawn. I struggled to keep my balance, heading for the spot I saw the spaceship land in the ivy.

"OUR LAUNCH WINDOW CLOSES IN SECONDS!" Ohm roared in my head, as if reading my mind.

"Wait! Wait!" Amp hollered in my head.

"Don't worry, guys. I'm ready. Prepare for lift-off!" I said. I plucked the spaceship from the ivy and snapped it into place on the ball thrower. Perfect fit.

Then I saw Amp running at me from the opposite direction, across the dimly lit grass, his arms held up like he wanted a hug.

That's when I knew he was going to miss me as much as I was going to miss him.

In one smooth, quick motion, I scooped him

up, gave him a trembling smile, and dropped him through the open hatch on Ohm's steaming and clicking spaceship.

This was not how I imagined our good-bye moment.

"ZACK, WAIT!" Olivia seemed to shout from a million miles away.

"NO TIME!" I croaked.

I adjusted my grip just as Amp's little head came poking up out of the still-open hatch. I gently pushed him back down with my index finger and closed the hatch with my palm. It clicked tightly into place.

The watch's alarm would surely stop at any moment.

"NO! WAIT!" Amp's voice shouted inside my head.

"Sorry, pal." I said. "We're out of time. I'll never forget you!"

The spaceship began to vibrate and hum.

Like a great hunter from mankind's distant past, I took three giant leaps forward across our dark backyard lawn, and executed the best throw of my life.

The dimly glowing spaceship shot high in the night sky and kept rising over the roof of our garage.

The beeping on my wrist stopped suddenly.

"We made it," I gurgled.

The flung spaceship seemed to rise impossibly high and fast. Just as I thought it might hit the top of its flight path, it expelled a huge blast of yellow fire—the secondary launch boosters!—which knocked me back a few steps like a punch to the chest.

The loud boom seemed to echo through the entire town. Every car alarm for three miles seemed to jump to life. Every dog in our neighborhood began barking and howling.

I felt Olivia step next to me. She put a hand on my shoulder. I didn't look over, as the hot tears that had been building up in my eyes now ran freely down my face.

We stood in silence and watched the spaceship rocket through the night sky, like a falling star that seemed to be falling up. The moon, which looked like a giant bowl of milk, seemed to be waiting for it.

I couldn't help it. The tears continued. I couldn't

stop the sobbing. I didn't care if Olivia saw me. I felt like I had just lost a family member.

Olivia, obviously feeling bad for me, wrapped an arm around my bouncing shoulders.

"Don't take it so hard, Zack. You had to do it. Besides, it wasn't your fault."

I sniffed. "My fault? What do you mean?"

"We still have time."

I blinked through tears. "Huh? Time for what?"

"To launch Amp, of course," she said, looking back.

And there sitting on the fence behind me was a bug-eyed Amp, peering up into the night sky with his mouth hanging open in shock.

And that's when, for the first time in my life, I fainted.

17

Grounded for Good?

I woke up on the dusty couch in Olivia's garage.

"Good. You're not dead," Olivia said softly.

I groaned. "What—?"

"You weigh more than two beached whales," Olivia said, sitting on a tall stool directly across from me. "I almost broke my back dragging you in here."

I sat upright, the crazy series of events coming back to me in an instant.

"Amp?!" I shouted, now seeing Amp sitting just like Olivia on a stool of his own.

"Honestly, I can't believe your ball thrower idea worked," Amp said, smiling.

"But I thought that was you I put in the spaceship!" I said, still trying to make sense of what had just happened in my backyard. "I thought you were trying to hug me."

Amp laughed. "Ohm is not a hugger."

"That was Ohm? I could have sworn that was you," I said.

Amp shook his head. "He was trying to stop you. After Olivia's mechanism failed, we were going to wait for the next launch opportunity twenty-eight

days from now."

Olivia shook her head. "Then, like a crazy zombie, you have to show up and take things into your own hands. That was amazing, Zack."

"You may have saved your fellow earthlings a lot of problems," Amp agreed.

I fell back into the couch cushion behind me. I winced at the pain in my back, probably from my fall from the ladder. "I did it," I said, staring blankly into the garage rafters above us. "And Ohm should be able to call off the invasion, too. I sort of just saved the world."

"Hopefully," Amp said. He sighed to explain. "Space travel is an inexact science. He might make it home in time—or he might not. I'd put the odds at about a million to one."

"Seriously?" I said, throwing up my arms. "How you guys have ever successfully invaded a planet is beyond me."

"Who says we have?" Amp said, confused.

"Well, look on the bright side, Zacky. At least you get to see Amp again," Olivia said with a shrug. "It was really sad when you didn't show up to say good-bye."

"Ohm tied me to my mattress with kite string and bungee cords. I had to escape like Houdini!"

"You did?" they both said at the same time.

Olivia shook her head in disbelief. "Wait, Ohm did say that you were tied up at the moment, but I didn't think he meant literally. I assumed you were in trouble again."

"He didn't want me getting in the way," I said. "He said Amp liked me too much."

"Really? I can't believe he said that," Amp said with a sly smile.

"Why weren't you on that ship?" I asked, still confused. "What if we can't fix your spaceship? You'll be stuck here."

"Neither of us were on that ship," Amp said. "Like I said, once Olivia's launcher failed, we called the launch off. We tried to tell you, but—"

"We'll fix your ship, Ampy," Olivia said firmly. "Especially now that we have an initial launch system that we know works. It's been field tested."

"What happened to your launcher?" I asked.

Olivia blew out a big breath. "It sort of fell apart. I ran out of time. My glue gun got clogged. I broke three springs. It actually fired off before I was ready."

"Fired off?" Amp complained. "It basically just snapped. I bit my tongue when Ohm's ship hit that tree." This made us all laugh, as Amp pulled on his tongue to show us the damage.

"Well, guys, that's enough fun for me for one night," Olivia said, standing up and yawning. "I don't want Grandpa to find my bed empty at this hour of the night. Plus, we're both going fishing in a couple of hours." She groaned and stretched.

"There is one great thing about all this," Amp said. "Zack and I can finish watching *The Mummy*. C'mon, let's go!"

I smiled, reached out, and held up my hand up for a high five. He gave me a high three, which was the best he could manage.

"You love that movie," I said.

"We can worry about getting me home tomorrow."

And with that, we headed back to my house.

His broken spaceship and everything else would have to wait till the morning.

We had a movie to finish.

THE END

Try It Yourself: Atlatl

Have you ever heard of the term *leverage*? As in, "We need to get a bit more leverage"? Zack cleverly uses a ball-throwing toy, usually used for chucking tennis balls for his dog, to get himself more leverage for throwing Ohm's ship into the air. You're probably already much more familiar with the concept of leverage than you think.

Levers are all around you. As Ohm points out in his note to the Erdian Council, a lever is basically a stick that pivots, or rotates, around a certain point. When we're thinking about the stick as a lever, rather than just a stick, we call that pivot point the *fulcrum*.

The door to your bedroom is a lever. The fulcrum, or the point that the lever pivots around, is the pin going through the hinges of the door. A teeter-totter on a playground is also a lever. Have you ever wondered what would happen if a really big person jumped onto the seat across from you? If the person were big enough, the teeter-totter might lever you right up into the air!

The Levers in Your Body

There are a few levers you use *every day*, even if you don't open a door or stop by the playground. Those levers are your arms and legs! Each joint—like your wrist joint or your shoulder joint—act as a *fulcrum* for those levers. Your hand and lower arm pivot around those joints, acting as levers.

The way the human body's levers are arranged make them very good for speedy movements because they're very long. Can you imagine if your end of the teeter-totter grew to double the length it started from? If a big kid jumped on the other end, you'd really go flying!

That's the same concept Zack takes advantage of when he uses his ball thrower to chuck Ohm's spaceship into the air. The ball thrower makes his arm—the lever that's throwing the ship—even longer than it was to begin with, giving the space-ship an extra boost.

Ancient Leverage-the Atlatl

Humans have been using leverage to throw things extra far for a lot longer than tennis ball chuckers have been around. In fact, the first examples of intentionally using leverage for this purpose can be traced back to nearly 30,000 years ago! The most famous example, however, was used by the Aztecs in the sixteenth century, and is called an *atlatl*. It's a fantastic example of how a simple tool can augment human capability in a really powerful way.

You can build your own atlatl using a few simple materials.

YOU WILL NEED: Some pieces of cardboard a few feet long (ideally with the corrugations running lengthwise), a roll of tape (like duct tape), scissors, a stick about as long as your forearm, a pen to decorate the cardboard ship, a piece of dish sponge to serve as a soft tip, and an adult to help you cut the materials.

Making the Ship

1. Lay the cardboard lengthwise along a countertop or other flat surface with a corner edge. Use the edge to fold the cardboard along its length, with about a 1-inch width.

115

2. Fold the cardboard a few times until you can wrap the cardboard around on itself, making a long skinny tube. It can be a triangle, a square, or even rolled into a circle. It doesn't have to be a perfect shape, but it should be long, skinny, and pretty straight. Once you have wrapped the cardboard into a tube, have a grown-up help you cut off any extra cardboard. Use the tape to hold it in the shape of a tube.

3. Make fins to help the ship fly straight. In ancient times, creating fins with feathers, like on an arrow, was called fletching. We'll use more cardboard to make ours. You can choose how you shape your fins. Ask an adult to help you cut them. Definitely decorate them—maybe by drawing Ohm's face on one!

4. Then tape two fins to the bottom of the ship so they stick out evenly on both sides like wings of a plane. Tape another fin to the top of the ship so it appears to have three equally sized fins.

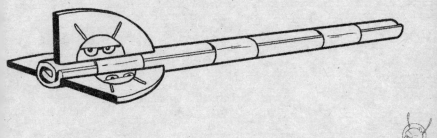

5. Cushion the front tip of the ship with something in case it hits anything delicate. You can use anything that's small and soft, but a piece of a dry, squishy kitchen sponge can work really well. With help from an adult, cut a little square out and tape it on the tip of the ship.

Building the Atlatl

1. Cut a small piece of cardboard in the shape that's shown in the picture. Cut it so that the cardboard can fold easily in half along one of the corrugation pieces. Fold the shape in half, and then tape it to the end of the stick.

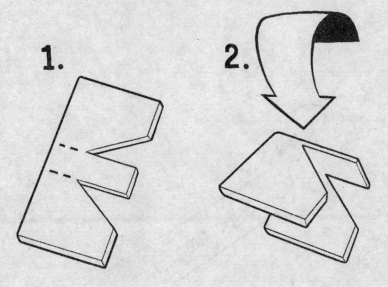

2. If you can't find a stick the right size, you can make your own using the same technique you used to make the dart.

3. Tape the folded cardboard shape, or hook, onto the atlatl with one half of the hook on each side. Be sure to tape it tightly, and consider reinforcing it further with some tape. During a good throw, it's likely to undergo some high forces!

4. You might want to add a little grip on the bottom of your atlatl so it's easier to hold on to during a throw. You can tape a piece of cardboard onto the bottom of the atlatl, or make up your own grip enhancement.

Launching Ohm Back Home:
Throwing with the Atlatl

1. Put the back end of the spaceship, where the fins are, into the atlatl's hook. Hang on to the atlatl's grip, and reach around the shaft with your thumb and fingers, using them to pinch the ship's long body and hold it in place parallel to the atlatl. You're ready to throw!

2. Throwing with the atlatl uses the same motion as throwing a baseball, so use exactly the same technique. The atlatl will naturally let go of the ship at the right time.

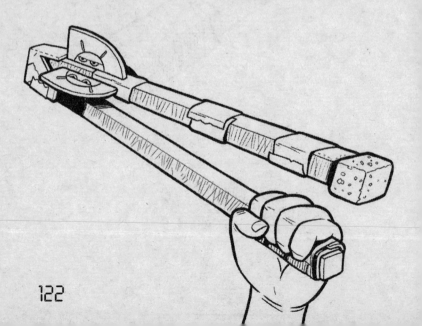

Experiment Time

You'll probably have some success to start off with, but here are some ways you can work on the design and your own throwing motion to get the most out of your atlatl project.

1. Aim at different angles. Try throwing in a more upward direction. Does the ship fly in the path you expected? How might you adjust the angle you're throwing at so that it flies along the trajectory you want?

2. Try a different length of ship. It helps to have a longer ship, because it's harder for a long spaceship to tilt itself in a different course from the one you started throwing it in.

3. Test a different length of atlatl. If a long lever is good, is a longer lever better? Try a few different lengths of atlatl to see which gives you the most leverage. Do different atlatls require different technique to throw effectively?

4. Try throwing at different speeds. An effective throw will combine raw power with good technique. You may want to experiment with a lower power throw that you can control better before adding additional throwing effort.

Safety Notes

- Do this experiment with an adult! The adult isn't there to do the experiment for you, and in fact he or she should let you do as much of it as you can. But make sure someone is available to help with the hard parts, like cutting the cardboard and choosing a safe place to throw.

- Choose a safe place to throw! It should be a wide-open area where there are no people, animals, or things that wouldn't like to get hit with a cardboard spaceship.

- Start small! As with any experiment, don't ramp up to full power right away. Start with light, easy throws that let you get the hang of it and develop control first. Then ramp up the power after you've developed some technique.

- Make sure there is nothing in front of you that can get hit! If you read the prior instructions, you might notice this is mentioned twice. That's because this is really important! Even through your cardboard spaceship doesn't weigh very much and has a soft tip from the sponge you taped on, you should never throw it toward anybody.

Digging Deeper

To learn more about the science behind the atlatl you've built, look into the physics of projectile motion. The most important thing about the atlatl is that it's a clever method of getting even more benefit out of the thing our appendages have evolved to be good at: speed.

Your arm is really strong, and also really fast. The cardboard spaceship you're throwing doesn't weigh very much—so you can throw it very easily. But because it weighs so little, your body is actually not able to maximize the amount of energy it can put into the projectile when throwing with just your normal arm. The atlatl enables your body to put more energy into the projectile by allowing you to bring it to an even higher release velocity (that means speed) than your hand can during a normal throw.

This can be illustrated by doing another experiment.

1. Hold the cardboard ship and prepare to throw it with just your hand. Have an adult hold your forearm steady and still, so you can only use your wrist to throw the ship. Your hand is functioning as the lever arm. Because the lever arm is so short, you won't be able to get the ship to a very high speed before you have to let go to throw it. The ship probably won't go very far.

2. Have the adult hold your upper arm steady while you throw. This way you're using your hand and forearm as the lever arm. Your lever arm is longer than last time. You'll be able to achieve a much higher speed than when you were throwing it with just your hand and wrist alone.

3. Throw it as you normally would, using the length of your hand, forearm, and upper arm. They become your lever arm and your shoulder joint becomes the fulcrum of this throwing lever. The ship should go pretty far!

4. Use your atlatl. The speed at the tip of the atlatl should be even higher than the speed you can make your hand go during a normal throw—meaning it'll go extra high in the air. It's that release velocity that matters, and you want it to be as high as possible. Maybe high enough to launch Ohm back into orbit. Be safe, and have fun!

Forces of Nature

01

What a Trip

"The answer is still no," Zack said, stuffing a pair of jeans into the canvas bag that usually held his baseball gear.

"Just think about it," Amp said from atop a pair of rolled-up wool socks that sat on Zack's desk.

"What part of 'no' are you not getting?" Zack asked. "The *n* or the *o* part? It's really a pretty simple word."

Amp stared off into space dreamily. "I've always wanted to go camping." He sighed.

"What?" Zack said, fixing his eyes on his tiny

1

alien roommate. "Yesterday you had never even heard of camping! Now, suddenly, it's your life-long goal? Give me a break, Short Pants."

"We Erdians are fast learners," Amp said with a proud shrug of his little blue shoulders. He folded his arms behind his head and nestled deeper into the sock. "Besides, what an adventure! The chance to battle the elements, the opportunity to encounter wild animals, the daily struggle to find food? Who would pass that up?"

"I already told you, we don't struggle to find food." Zack groaned, pulling a fistful of underwear from an open drawer and tossing it into his bag. "We bring about five hundred pounds of food with us. We're not exactly hunting down beavers with bows and arrows."

Amp sat up and grabbed his antennas with excitement. "And to sleep on the ground in that little cloth house held up by sticks."

"You mean a tent," Zack said flatly.

"Yes!" Amp said, snapping his fingers. "A tent! I want to sleep in a tent."

"Forget it," Zack said, sitting on the corner of his unmade bed and holding his head in his hands.

"Quit bugging me about this, okay? You know my family can never know you're here. They'd freak out if they ever saw you. Call the park ranger. Call the cops. Call the government. Not to mention you've still got a little alien invasion to stop. Remember the whole reason you came to this planet in the first place? You don't want the Erdian Army to arrive only to find their lead scout napping in the woods."

"Come on, a camping trip might be just the thing I need to get the creative juices flowing again."

"It's too risky. If anyone else sees you, they'll take you away and dissect you like a frog."

"But look at the size of me," Amp said, standing up and doing a sort of jumping-jack motion. "I'm so little, they'd never see me. Plus, you know how good I am at staying out of sight."

Zack looked over at Amp and shook his head at his friend's energy.

His family had gone on an annual camping trip for the last three years, and each year had been a disaster. The McGee family just wasn't the outdoorsy type. But every year Zack's dad insisted they go. And every year, a perfectly good three-day weekend was ruined.

Amp fell onto his belly and pressed his face into the fluffy socks. "I promise if you take me with you to the Crooked Forest," his muffled voice begged, "you'll never know I was even there. I'll be like a ninja."

"It's not called the Crooked Forest," Zack said, rolling his eyes. "It's called Twisted Grove State Park."

"Yes! That's it. I want to see the ghost, too," Amp said, rolling onto his back and staring up at the ceiling. "I've never seen a ghost."

"There's no ghost," Zack sighed. "That's just a story people made up."

"You told me the outlaw Nasty Ned hid his stolen gold in that forest over a hundred years ago, but could never find the spot where he buried it. Now his ghost wanders through the trees at night trying to find it."

"I was just reading you that stuff from the back of the park's map," Zack explained.

Amp sat up. "The anger from Nasty Ned's ghost made all those trees crooked. That's just so exciting."

4

"But it's not true! It's just something they wrote to make the campgrounds sound mysterious to tourists. It's just a bunch of trees that got bent out of shape. It's no big deal."

"Watch this," Amp said, and he disappeared from sight. "See, nobody will see me," his voice explained. "I'll be invisible. Now let's go hug some trees and see ghosts in the Crooked Forest!"

Zack pinched the bridge of his nose in frustration.

He knew all too well about the Erdian mind trick that enabled Amp to stop your brain from seeing him. The way Amp explained it, he could make your brain forget you were seeing him at the same instant you were seeing him. Zack had trained himself to block the mind trick when he wanted to, but now he just stared at the empty space above the sock.

"Forget it," Zack said, yanking the sock off the desk and stuffing it in his bag. He heard Amp give an invisible cry and then appear just as he crashed onto the desk.

"Ouch!" Amp yelled. "That was incredibly rude."

"See, you can't always be invisible," Zack said

with a chuckle, zipping up his bag and heading toward the door. "Under the bed are enough Ritz Crackers and SweeTarts to last you a month. I'll be back late on Monday night, okay? Are we good?"

"But I'll be so bored," Amp whined, rubbing the back of his head.

"Just stay in here and out of trouble," Zack said and closed his door.

Alone in the hallway, Zack pressed on the door to make sure it was securely shut, sighed, shook his head, and headed downstairs.

There was one more thing he had to do before leaving.

02

The Ol' Switcheroo

"Jimmy has pinkeye," Zack's little brother, Taylor, reported when Zack dropped his bag at the front door. "He can't go camping with us."

"No biggie," Zack said. "More room in the kids' tent."

"But Jimmy always comes with us," Taylor moaned. "He just called. Both his eyes are glued shut with pus."

"Gross! Thanks for sharing, Taylor," Zack said.

Taylor sighed. "This will be our worst camping trip ever."

Zack shrugged. "I'm not so sure. The bar is set pretty low."

"Oh, stop it, you two," Zack's mom said, rolling out a plastic cooler stuffed with ice and food. "C'mon, Zack, bring this and your bag out to Dad.

Olivia is helping him put everything on top of the car."

"Olivia? Why?" Zack asked.

Helping Dad tie down the tents and bags was usually his job. And while Olivia was his best friend and next-door neighbor, sometimes she helped out around his house a little too often, which tended to make him look lazy by comparison.

Mom brushed Zack's hair from his face with her fingers. "Since Jimmy couldn't go with us, I asked Olivia to come instead. It'll be so fun."

Zack pulled away from his mom. "What?!"

Zack had planned on having Olivia keep an eye on Amp while he was gone. She was the only other person on the planet who knew about Amp, so her going on this trip threw a major wrench into his plans.

Plus, when Zack thought about the close quarters of a tent, camping with Olivia might be a little . . . embarrassing. He flapped his arms, trying to think of something to say. "Mom, I can't sleep in a tent with Olivia. She's a girl. It's just weird!"

"Yeah, Zack likes to fart when he camps,"

Taylor said. "Nobody should be subjected to his weaponized toots."

"Don't be crude, honey," Mom said to Taylor with a tsk-tsk. "Zack can't help it if he has a sensitive system."

"I don't have a sensitive system," Zack said. "It's just that . . . I don't know. It's just weird, Mom."

What Zack couldn't say was that, while he knew Olivia would make this camping trip a lot more fun, the thought of leaving Amp unsupervised for a whole three-day weekend made him nervous. Amp was like a disaster magnet.

"Zack also likes to sleep in his underwear," Taylor said. "Now he can't."

"That's not true," Zack said.

Mom continued to try to fix up Zack's hair. "Olivia and I can sleep in the small tent, and you, Taylor, and your father can sleep in the big tent."

"Dad! He snores like a volcano," Zack protested.

"Volcanoes don't snore," Taylor said, shaking his head at his brother's lack of basic science knowledge. "But they do sort of burp. Mostly water vapor and carbon dioxide. But also lots of different sulfur compounds. It's a long list and varies by volcano."

Zack stared at his brother like he was the alien in the house, and then began flapping his arms again. "It's bad enough that Taylor laughs in his sleep, now I get snoring on top of it?"

"I don't laugh in my sleep!" Taylor shouted, apparently insulted at being accused of sleep-laughing.

"She's already coming," Mom said with a firm nod. "Now let's have fun, you two."

Zack looked out the window and could see Olivia on top of the car, helping Zack's dad thread twine through the handles of various suitcases and tent bags.

Olivia *was* also going to feed Mr. Jinxy and walk Smokey while they were gone. Now somebody else would have to come into the house to take care of the cat and the dog, further risking the accidental discovery of Amp.

Zack closed his eyes and shook his head slowly. Camping had always seemed inconvenient, but this year there was so much more at stake.

Zack had a bad feeling about this trip.

He wished he were the one who had come down with pinkeye.

But he was not the lucky type.